Waddling

written by Pam Holden
illustrated by Michael Cashmore-Hingley

At the farm there was one animal who made the others cross because she thought she was the smartest one. "I must be the smartest animal on the whole farm," Duck told the other animals, "because I can move around the farm in many ways to see what is happening. I can walk through the green fields just like you," she told Cow and Horse. "When I get tired of walking, I can fly up into the sky."

Cow and Horse were happy walking through the fields,
but they wished Duck would stop quacking and leave
them alone. "You are so lucky. Show us how you can
fly," said Cow and Horse. Duck flapped her wings and
proudly flew away, quacking as she went.

4

"I'm the smartest animal on the whole farm," Duck told Eagle and Hawk. "I can fly in the blue sky just like you, but when I get tired of flying, I can land on the lake or the pond or the river for a swim."

6

Eagle and Hawk loved flying high up to the clouds above the farm, but they didn't like listening to Duck. "We can't land on water!" they told her. "Show us how you do that." Duck flew away and landed smoothly on the pond.

Duck swam around on the pond until she found Frog and Fish. "I am much luckier than you," she told them, "because I can go more places than you can. I have been walking and flying already this morning, and now I can swim like you."

8

Frog and Fish were very happy swimming in the pond, but they didn't want Duck quacking at them about how smart she was. "You are so clever," they told her. "Show us how you can fly away." Duck took off from the pond and flew high into the air, quacking proudly.

Duck landed beside Rabbit. "Do you know that I am the
only animal on the whole farm who can fly and swim and
walk?" asked Duck. "You can't even walk, can you?"
"I just hop and run," said Rabbit. "I don't need to walk.
When you fly, you can't fly as high and far as Eagle and
Hawk. When you swim, you can't swim deep and fast like
Fish and Frog. And when you walk..." Rabbit began to
laugh. He laughed so much that he couldn't talk.

10

"I wish you would tell me what is so funny about
when I walk," said Duck crossly.
But Rabbit just kept laughing and giggling.
"I'll show you by the river," he said. "Follow me."

At the river, he told Duck to walk beside the water and see for herself how she looked when she walked. She walked slowly along the riverbank, looking at herself in the water. Poor Duck could see that she didn't walk like Cow or Horse. She didn't like the funny way she looked when she walked.

Rabbit hopped along behind her, laughing loudly.
"You look even funnier from the back," he told her.
"That isn't a walk at all — it's a waddle."
Duck wished that she hadn't said such silly things
to the other animals. She felt sorry that she had
thought she was the smartest.

14

"I am lucky that I can swim on the top of the water," said Duck. "I'm lucky that I can take off and land on the water when I fly. I know now that I can't walk like Cow and Horse, but I can waddle around the farm." After that Duck was happy to live quietly on the farm with the other animals.

16